the MYSTERY of the LOVE LIST

BY **SARAH GLENN MARSH**

ILLUSTRATED BY **ISHAA LOBO**

VIKING

VIKING

An imprint of Penguin Random House LLC, New York

First published in the United States of America by Viking,
an imprint of Penguin Random House LLC, 2022

Text copyright © 2022 by Sarah Glenn Marsh
Illustrations copyright © 2022 by Ishaa Lobo Illustration Ltd.

Viking & colophon are registered trademarks of Penguin Random House LLC.

Visit us online at penguinrandomhouse.com.

Library of Congress Cataloging-in-Publication Data is available.

Manufactured in China

ISBN 9780593352212

1 3 5 7 9 10 8 6 4 2

TOPL

Design by Opal Roengchai
Text set in Neutrace 2 Text
The illustrations were done digitally using a range of textured brushes.

To Dawn, who will always be my valentine
—S. G. M

To my lovely and supportive family
—I. L.

When you're the only porcupine
in your class, you stand out.
Just ask Pippa.

Because sometimes,
even in a crowded forest,
you still get lonely.

Today's Art Lesson:
Making a
Love List! ♡

Three days before Valentine's Day, Mr. Tod gives his class an art project. "Today, you will each make a 'love list.' This is a list of things that take up room in your heart."

Pippa would rather read her newest mystery book.

After Art, she goes to her usual lunch table.
But suddenly, she's not hungry.

Love is in the air . . .
. . . and it stinks.

She must be the only one in
the whole school without a
best friend to share her
heart-shaped pizza with.

On her way to Music,
something sticks to Pippa's quills.

Love List
♥ Berry Berry Twigs cereal
♥ The Beastly Boys
♥ Mysteries
♥ Deer, Deer, Moose
♥ Baking
♥ Pippa
♥ Painting
♥ Swimming
♥ Pink

Somebody loves her!

Somebody is a lot like her.

Somewhere in these halls, she has a best-friend-in-waiting!

Who could it be?

There's nothing Pippa loves more than a mystery.

By morning, she has a plan.
She'll try every activity on the list
and interview those who join in.
Maybe they'll have something else
in common? She gathers supplies
to be the perfect detective.

Beastly Boys

The list of names in her notebook is four pages long by lunchtime!
It's a good thing she has plenty of other ways to narrow the suspects.
"Nice shirt, Pippa!" someone calls when she gets to school.
"Really cool," squeaks Mitzie, the quietest mouse in class.
Pippa knows everyone loves the Beastly Boys as much as she does,
so that's not much of a clue.

At recess, she starts a game of Deer, Deer, Moose and writes down the names of each player. As they run and laugh, she opens some Berry Berry Twigs cereal, but no one is hungry. Five people in the group are wearing pink, so that isn't much help either. Pippa sighs. At least the game is fun.

Lucky for her, there are still two days until Valentine's.
But no matter what she tries, or how many of her
classmates she interviews . . .

. . . she's no closer to finding her new best friend.

No one she talked to while swimming was a fan
of the Beastly Boys, and no one in Art was
interested in the latest Sherlock Gnomes mystery.
She's running out of suspects—and time.

With one day left until Valentine's, she curls up
next to the oldest tree in the forest and sighs.

On Valentine's morning,
Pippa looks through her photos again.
She followed the clues from the love list,
but she's sure she missed something.
Or someone.

Mitzie is in every one of her pictures, but she was so quiet that Pippa forgot to write her name in her notebook. Could her mystery friend have been right under her nose all this time?

Pippa has an idea. Someone as shy as Mitzie might hide when approached, but maybe there's another way to show her that Pippa solved the mystery and wants to be friends.

With just a few minutes left before school, she gets to work.

Before Art, she adds one final
clue and slips her new mystery
into Mitzie's desk.

And waits.

At lunch, as Pippa looks for Mitzie,
someone slides a book toward her.
It's the latest Sherlock Gnomes,
and inside is a note.

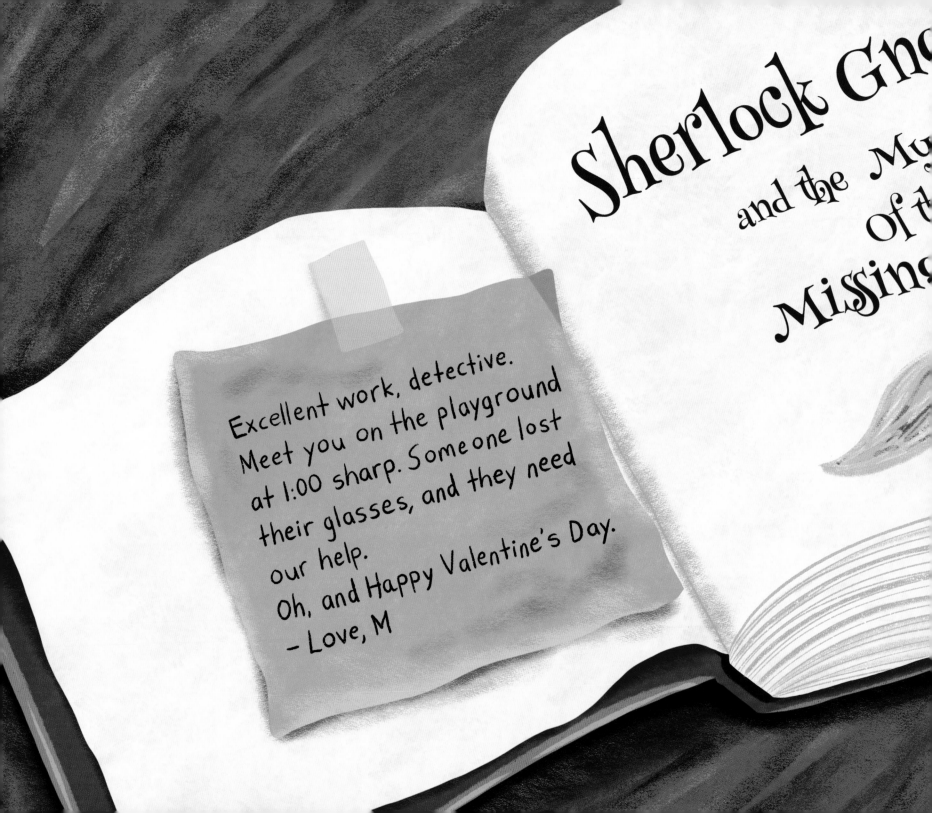

Pippa smiles and turns to a fresh page in her notebook. Case closed.